a Little Golden Book® Collection

Farm Tales

 A GOLDEN BOOK • NEW YORK

A GOLDEN BOOK • NEW YORK

Compilation copyright © 2007 by Random House, Inc.
The Shy Little Kitten copyright © 1946, renewed 1973 by Random House, Inc.
The Boy With a Drum copyright © 1969, renewed 1997 by Random House, Inc.
The Animals of Farmer Jones copyright © 1942, 1953, renewed 1970, 1981 by Random House, Inc.
Baby Farm Animals © 1953, 1958, renewed 1981, 1987 by Random House, Inc.
The Jolly Barnyard copyright © 1950, renewed 1978 by Random House, Inc.
The Fuzzy Duckling copyright © 1949, renewed 1977 by Random House, Inc.
Mrs. Mooley copyright © 1973 by Random House, Inc.
A Name for Kitty copyright ©1948, renewed 1976 by Random House, Inc.
A Day on the Farm copyright © 1960, renewed 1988 by Random House, Inc.
All rights reserved. Published in the United States by Golden Books, an imprint of Random House Children's Books,
a division of Random House, Inc., New York.
Originally published in slightly different form in 2004 by Random House, Inc. GOLDEN BOOKS, A GOLDEN BOOK,
A LITTLE GOLDEN BOOK, the G colophon, and the distinctive gold spine are registered trademarks of Random House, Inc.
The Shy Little Kitten is a registered trademark of Random House, Inc.
www.goldenbooks.com
www.randomhouse.com/kids
Educators and librarians, for a variety of teaching tools, visit us at
www.randomhouse.com/teachers
Library of Congress Control Number: 2006924403
ISBN: 978-0-375-83942-9
20 19 18 17 16 15 14 13
PRINTED IN CHINA   First Random House Edition 2007

Contents

The Shy Little Kitten • 1

By Cathleen Schurr   *Illustrated by* Gustaf Tenggren

The Boy With a Drum • 25

By David L. Harrison   *Illustrated by* Eloise Wilkin

The Animals of Farmer Jones • 49

Illustrated by Richard Scarry

Baby Farm Animals • 70

By Garth Williams

The Jolly Barnyard • 93

By Annie North Bedford   *Illustrated by* Tibor Gergely

The Fuzzy Duckling • 117

By Jane Werner Watson   *Illustrated by* Alice and Martin Provensen

Mrs. Mooley • 141

By Jack Kent

A Name for Kitty • 166

By Phyllis McGinley   *Illustrated by* Feodor Rojankovsky

A Day on the Farm • 189

By Nancy Fielding Hulick   *Illustrated by* J. P. Miller

THE SHY LITTLE KITTEN

Way up in the hayloft of an old red barn lived a mother cat and her new baby kittens. There were five bold and frisky little roly-poly black and white kittens, and *one* little striped kitten who was very, very shy.

One day, the five bold little roly-poly black and white kittens and the one little roly-poly striped kitten who was very, very shy all sat down and washed their faces and paws with

busy little red tongues. They smoothed down their soft baby fur and stroked their whiskers and followed their mother down the ladder from the hayloft—jump, jump, jump!

Then off they marched, straight out of the cool, dark barn, into the warm sunshine. How soft the grass felt under their paws! The five bold and frisky little kittens rolled over in the grass and kicked up their heels with joy.

But the shy little striped kitten just stood off by herself at the very end of the line.

That was how she happened to see the earth push up in
a little mound right in front of her. Then—*pop!*—up came
a pointed little nose. The nose belonged to a chubby mole.

"Good morning!" said the mole, as friendly as you please. "Won't you come for a walk with me?"

"Oh," said the shy little kitten. She looked shyly over her shoulder.

But the mother cat and her five bold and frisky kittens had disappeared from sight.

So the shy little kitten went walking with the chubby mole. Soon they met a speckled frog sitting near the pond.

"My, what big eyes he has!" whispered the shy little kitten. But the frog had sharp ears, too.

He chuckled. "My mouth is much bigger. Look!" And the frog opened his great cave of a mouth.

The mole and the kitten laughed and laughed until their sides ached.

When the kitten stopped laughing and looked around, the frog had vanished. On the pond, ripples spread out in great silver circles.

"I really should be getting back to my mother and the others," said the shy little kitten, "but I don't know where to find them."

"I'll show you," said a strange voice. And out of the bushes bounded a shaggy black puppy.

"Oh, thank you," said the shy little kitten. "Good-bye, mole."

So off they went together, the shy little kitten and the shaggy puppy dog. The little kitten, of course, kept her eyes shyly on the ground.

But the shaggy puppy stopped to bark, "Woof, woof," at a red squirrel in a tree. He was full of mischief.

"Chee, chee, chee," the squirrel chattered back. And she dropped a hickory nut right on the puppy's nose. She was very brave.

"Wow, wow, wow," barked the mischievous puppy, and off they went toward the farm.

Soon they came bounding out of the woods, and there before them stretched the farmyard.

"Here we are," said the shaggy puppy dog.

So down the hillside they raced, across the bridge above the brook, and straight on into the farmyard.

In the middle of the farmyard was the mother cat with her five bold and frisky little black and white kittens. In a flash, the mother cat was beside her shy kitten, licking her all over with a warm red tongue.

"Where have you been?" she cried. "We're all ready to start on a picnic."

The kittens scampered busily around, sampling everything. They turned up their noses at the chickens' tasty beetles, but they tried the carrots and cabbage, the cracked wheat and tree bark. They all liked best the mash from the pig's big trough.

Yum, yum, yum! How good it all was! Everyone was just beginning to feel comfortable and drowsy, when suddenly the frog jumped straight into the air, eyes almost popping out of his head.

"Help! Run!" he cried.

The frog made a leap for the brook.

Everyone scrambled after him and tumbled into the water.

"What is it?" asked the shy little kitten.

"A bee!" groaned the frog. "I bit a bee!"

Then they saw that one side of his mouth was puffed up like a green balloon.

Everybody laughed. They couldn't help it. Even the frog laughed. They all looked so funny as they climbed out of the brook.

The shy little kitten stood off to one side. She felt so good that she turned a backward somersault, right there in the long meadow grass. "This is the best day ever," said the shy little kitten.

The Boy With a Drum

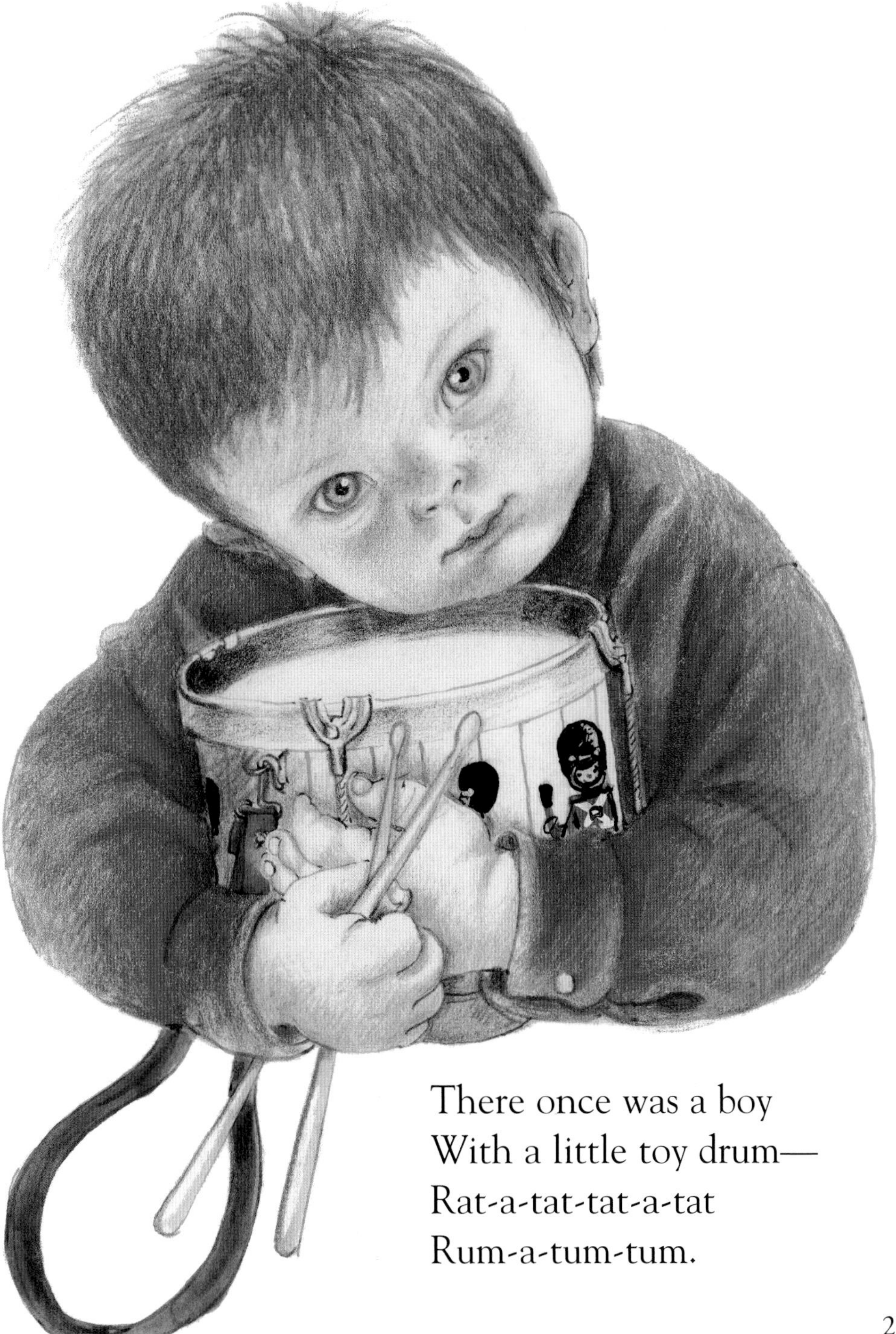

There once was a boy
With a little toy drum—
Rat-a-tat-tat-a-tat
Rum-a-tum-tum.

One day he went marching
And played on his drum—
Rat-a-tat-tat-a-tat
Rum-a-tum-tum.

Soon he was joined
By a friendly old cat—
Rum-a-tum-tum-a-tum
Rat-a-tat-tat.

Next they were joined
By a green spotted frog
Who sat by the road
On an old brown log.

And then they were joined
By a big yellow dog
Who marched down the road
With the green spotted frog.

They marched by a field,
They marched by a house—
And were joined by a cow
And a furry brown mouse.

37

They marched by a horse
Who was pulling a plow,
And he trotted behind them
And followed the cow.

39

Next they were joined
By a big white duck
And an old mother chicken
With a cluck-cluck-cluck.

And a pig and a goose
And a billy goat, too,
And a big red rooster
With a cock-a-doodle-doo.

And they all went marching
With a rat-a-tat-tat,
The boy with his drum
And the big friendly cat.

The horse and the cow
And the mouse and the dog,
The duck and the chicken
And the pig and the frog.

The goose and the rooster
And a billy goat, too,
With a baaa, honk, quack,
And a cock-a-doodle-doo,

Oink, bow-wow, and a
Moo-moo-moo,
Neigh, cluck, squeak,
And a mew-mew-mew.

They all marched away
To the top of a hill—
If they haven't stopped marching,
They'll be marching still.

RICHARD SCARRY'S
the ANIMALS of FARMER JONES

It is supper time on the farm.
The animals are very hungry.
But where is Farmer Jones?

The horse stamps in his stall.
"Nei-g-hh, nei-g-hh," says the horse.

"I want my supper."
But where is Farmer Jones?

The cow jangles her bell.

"Moo, moo," says the cow.

"I am very hungry."

But where is Farmer Jones?

The sheep sniff around the barn.
"Ba-a-a, ba-a-a-a," say the sheep.
"We're waiting for supper."
But where is Farmer Jones?

"Cluck, cluck," say the chickens.
"Give us our supper."
But where is Farmer Jones?

The dog runs about barking.
"Wuff, wuff," says the dog.
"I want my meal."
But where is Farmer Jones?

The cat rubs against a post.
"Me-o-w, me-o-w," says the cat.
"My dish is empty."
But where is Farmer Jones?

The pigs snuffle in the trough.
"Oink, oink," say the pigs.
"There's nothing to eat."
But where is Farmer Jones?

Farmer Jones is out in the field.
"Six o'clock!" says Farmer Jones.
"It's supper time!"
He goes to get food for the animals.

He gives oats to the horse.
"Nei-g-hh, nei-g-hh," says the horse.
"Thank you, Farmer Jones."

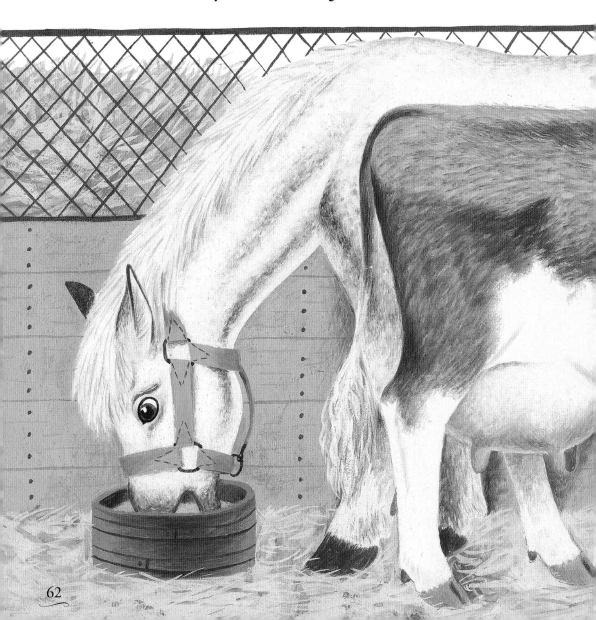

He gives grain to the cow.
"Moo, moo," says the cow.
"Thank you, Farmer Jones."

He gives turnips to the sheep.
"Ba–a–a, ba–a–a–a," say the sheep.
"Thank you, Farmer Jones."

He gives corn to the chickens.
"Cluck, cluck," say the chickens.
"Thank you, Farmer Jones."

He gives bones to the dog.

"Wuff, wuff," says the dog.

"Thank you, Farmer Jones."

He gives milk to the cat.

"Me-e-o-w, me-e-o-w," says the cat.

"Thank you, Farmer Jones."

He gives mash to the pigs.
But the pigs don't say thank you.
The pigs don't say anything.
They are much too busy eating.

"I am hungry, too," says Farmer Jones.
And off he goes for his supper.
Good–bye, Farmer Jones.

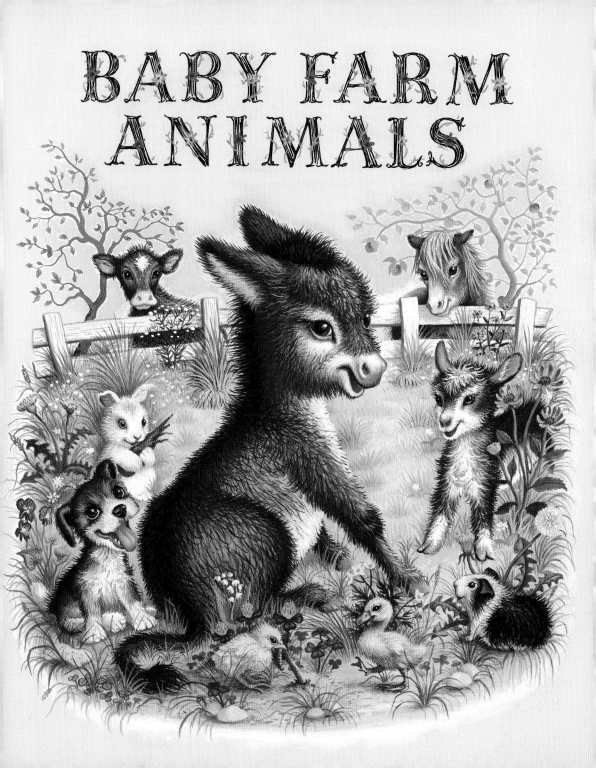

BABY FARM ANIMALS

Baby Sheep is called a lamb. He likes to run in the grass that grows in the meadow.

Baby Cats are called kittens. They love playing on the farm. At night the farmer gives them cow's milk, and they curl up together in the big red barn.

Baby Rabbit lives in a hutch, which is her tiny little house. She sniffs noses with the kittens and puppies because they are all friends.

Baby Guinea Pigs also have a hutch. Have you ever seen a guinea pig's tail?

"That rabbit has been up to some mischief," says the brown guinea pig.

Baby Donkey loves to eat juicy carrots. He is
sitting down because he is tired. Somebody is trying
to make him stand up and follow those carrots tied
on the end of a stick.

"I know that trick," he says.

Baby Ducks are called ducklings. They swim in the pond with their wide, webbed feet.

"Why don't you come for a swim?" they ask the little chicks.

Baby Chickens are called chicks. They cannot swim.

"Mother says we must look for worms and stay out of the water," they reply.

Baby Pigs are called piglets. They love clean straw to sleep on. A piglet digs with his nose, which is called a snout. If you pick him up or chase him, he will squeal for his mother: "Help, help, help!"

Baby Dogs are called puppies. They stay in the stable, close to the horses. They growl and bark at strangers. They pretend that the shoe is a big cat. They growl and bark at it, too.

Baby Goats are called kids, just as little boys and girls are. They try to knock each other down by butting their heads together. Their father has horns and a pointed beard.

Baby Swans are called cygnets. Now they are covered with smoke-colored down, but soon they will have pure white feathers and long, long necks.

Baby Goose is called a gosling. She will be a big gray goose someday. See her brother with his head under the water. He is looking for something to eat.

Baby Horse we call a foal. She could walk the same day she was born. Now, after a week, she gallops. When she is two years old, she will be a beautiful horse, and she will be able to carry a rider on her back. Perhaps she will even win a race.

Baby Pony is taking Kitten and Puppy for a ride. He is a Shetland pony, so he will not grow very much bigger.

Baby Cow is called a calf. She says, "Moooo! It is time for lunch."

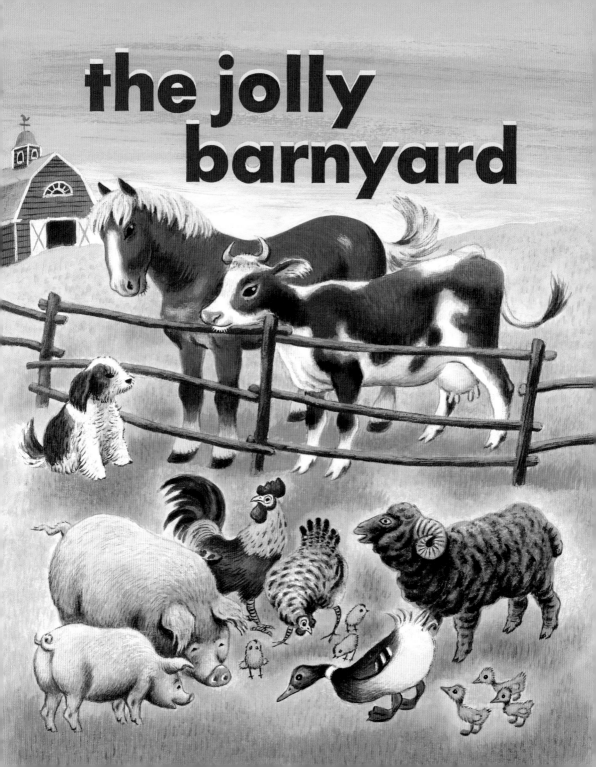

the jolly barnyard

Said Farmer Brown, "Tra-la, tra-lee!
Today is my birthday, lucky me!
I'll give my animals a treat—
for each, what he likes best to eat."

First he took a pan of oats, of course,
to the baby colt and the mother horse.

For the cow and calf he set corn down.
"'Cause today is my birthday,"
said Farmer Brown.

The big white ram and the fat black sheep
ate all the grain in a great big heap.

The gobbling turkey ate and ate until
he had to admit he'd eaten his fill.

The chickens and rooster got their food—
enough for all their hungry brood.

And so did the duck, and so did the drake
and the ducklings down beside the lake.

The dog got bones to bury and to chew.

The cat got milk—and the kitten did, too.

When all the animals had been fed,
Farmer Brown left, and the spotted cow said:

"Kind Farmer Brown! What would you say
we could do for him on his birthday?"

"We'll pull his loads smoothly, with never a jolt,"
said the big brown horse and her little brown colt.

"Moo-oo, I'll give him lots of milk," said the cow.
Said her calf, "I will, too, someday, somehow!"

"Baa-aa, we'll give him wool," said the sheep.
"For our fleece is soft and warm and deep."

"Gobble!" said the turkey. "As well as I am able,
I'll decorate his Thanksgiving table."

"Cluck! I will give him eggs," said the hen.
Said the rooster, "I'll wake him in the
mornings, then."

"Quack! He can have duck eggs," said the duck.
"And I'll swim on his pond," said the drake,
"for luck."

"Bow-wow!" said the dog. "I'll guard his house both night and day, but most of all when he's away!"

"Mew! We'll catch his mice," said the cat.
"We're good hunters," said the kitten.
"Farmer Brown will tell you that."

Inside the farmhouse was another treat—
a beautiful birthday cake to eat.
What a happy birthday for Farmer Brown!

The Fuzzy
Duckling

Early one bright morning
a small fuzzy duckling went for a walk.
He walked through the sunshine.
He walked through the shade.

In the long striped shadows
that the cattails made
he met two frisky colts.

"Hello," said the duckling.
"Will you come for a walk with me?"

But the two frisky colts would not.

So on went the little duckling,
on over the hill.

There he found three spotted calves,
all resting in the shade.
"Hello," said the duckling.
"Will you come for a walk with me?"

But the sleepy calves would not.
So on went the duckling.

He met four noisy turkeys

and five white geese

and six lively lambs
with thick soft fleece.

But no one would come for a walk
with the fuzzy duckling.
So on he went, all by his lone.

He met seven playful puppies

and eight hungry pigs.
"Won't you come for a walk with me?"
asked the fuzzy duckling.

"You had better walk straight home,"
said the pigs.
"Don't you know it's suppertime?"

"Oh," said the duckling. "Thank you."
But which way was home?

Just as he began to feel quite unhappy,
he heard a sound in the rushes nearby . . .
and out waddled nine fuzzy ducklings
with their big mother duck.

"At last," said the mother duck.
"Here is our lost baby duckling."

"Get in line," called the other ducklings.
"We're going home for supper."

So the lost little duckling joined the line,
and away went the ten little ducklings,
home for supper.

"This is the best way to go for a walk,"
said the happy little, fuzzy little duck.

There was something on the floor of the barn. Mrs. Mooley went over to see what it was.

"Why," she said, "it's the book the farmer's little boy was reading. He must have dropped it."

Mrs. Mooley couldn't read, but she enjoyed looking at the pictures.

There was a picture of three men in a tub. There was a picture of an old woman who lived in a shoe.

There was a picture of a *cow jumping over the moon!*

"What fun!" cried Mrs. Mooley. She gave a little jump just for practice.

Mrs. Mooley came down
with a jolt that shook the
whole barn.

"Hey!" squawked the hen. "You're jostling my eggs! What do you think you're doing?"

"I'm practicing," said Mrs. Mooley. "I'm going to jump over the moon."

"Jump over the moon?" repeated the hen. *"Kut kut kahawww,"* she cackled. She laughed so hard, she hatched two of her eggs.

The pigeon in the loft laughed at Mrs.
Mooley.

The mouse in the straw laughed at
Mrs. Mooley.

"What's so funny?" the goose wanted
to know. They could hardly stop giggling
long enough to tell her. Finally they
gasped out the news.

"Honk haaaa kahonk!" The goose laughed so hard, she lost three tail feathers.

The goose told the duck.

"*Quaaaack!*" laughed the duck,
and told the horse.

The horse laughed so hard, he
got the hiccups.

"What's going on?" asked the pig.

"Mrs. Mooley *hic!* says she's going to *hic!* jump over the *hic!* moon," the horse told the pig.

The pig laughed so hard, he flopped into a mud puddle—which was where he planned to be, anyway.

When he came up for air, he told the goat about Mrs. Mooley.

The goat laughed.
The pig laughed.
The horse laughed.
The duck laughed.
The goose laughed.
The mouse and the pigeon laughed.
The hen and her chicks laughed.

They all laughed at
Mrs. Mooley until it
was bedtime.

All of the animals went to sleep—except Mrs. Mooley. She was out in the barnyard, jumping up and down.

"All it takes is determination," she said to herself, "and a little practice!"

All night long Mrs. Mooley jumped and jumped. And the moon shone down from high above her.

Mrs. Mooley was still jumping when a faint light in the eastern sky told that morning was coming.

The moon began to sink in the west. Its trip across the sky was ending.

The cock crowed, and one by one the animals woke up.

The moon was so low that it seemed to be sitting
on the ground. In a few minutes it would be gone.
Mrs. Mooley had time for one last jump.

It was her highest jump yet.

The animals saw the moon sitting on the ground. They saw Mrs. Mooley jump high in the air. They saw Mrs. Mooley *jump over the moon!*

"She *did* it!" screeched the hen. She was so excited, she hatched another egg.

The goose was so excited,
she lost another tail feather.
The horse was so excited,
his hiccups came back.
And the pig flopped into
the mud puddle again.

"You *did* it, Mrs. Mooley!" they all shouted at once. "You jumped over the moon!"

"All it takes is determination," said Mrs. Mooley, "and a little practice."

"I think I'll jump over the sun next," Mrs. Mooley went on. "No cow has ever done that before."

"Jump over the *sun*?" oinked the pig, and he fell back into the mud puddle. But only because he wanted to.

Nobody laughed at Mrs. Mooley this time.

"And after I jump over the sun, who knows?" said
Mrs. Mooley. "There are a lot of stars and planets
to jump over."

"Do you really think you could?" asked the horse.

    "Why not?" said Mrs. Mooley, and she gave a
tired sigh as she lay down in the hay. "All it takes
is determination and . . ."
    Mrs. Mooley's eyes blinked shut.
    She was fast asleep.

". . . and a little practice," said the hen, who
didn't like anything left unfinished.

A NAME
FOR
Kitty

Once, on a farm in the country, there lived a little boy who was given a brand-new kitty to be his very own. But she had no name and the little boy didn't know what to call her.

So he went to his mother and asked, "Mother, what shall I call my kitty?"

Now his mother was busy icing a cake and she gave the little boy the beater to lick.

"Why don't you call her 'Tiger'?"

"Oh, no," said the little boy, "I can't call her 'Tiger.' She's not that big."

So he went to find his father.

"Father," he asked, "what shall I call my kitty?"
Now his father was busy mending a fence and he gave
the little boy a hammer to hold while he put a board
in place.

"Why don't you call her 'Shoe-leather,' because she's bound to be always underfoot?"

"Oh, no!" cried the little boy. "That name's too long."

So he turned back to the house to find his grandfather.

His grandfather was sitting on the porch and he wasn't busy at all.

"Grandfather," asked the little boy, "what shall I call my kitty?"

"Wait a jiffy until I get my Thinking Cap," said his grandfather.

And he went inside to get his bright red Thinking Cap. "Why don't you call her 'Joseph,' because he had a coat of many colors?"

"But 'Joseph' is a boy's name and this is a girl kitty," said the little boy.

So he went to the stile and he climbed right over, and he asked of the cow who was nibbling at the clover, "Cow, what shall I call my kitty?"

"Mooo," lowed the cow, shaking her horn at a
butterfly. "Moo, moo-ooooo."

"Moo!" said the little boy. "That's no name for a kitty."

So he hurried to the barnyard as fast as he was able,
and he asked of the horse, at dinner in the stable,
"Horse, what shall I call my kitty?"

"Neigh," whinnied the horse, politely looking up from his oats. "Neigh, neighhhhh."

"Neigh!" exclaimed the little boy. "*That's* no name for a kitty."

So he walked by the garden, all alone, and he asked
of the dog who was digging up a bone,
"Dog, what shall I call my kitty?"
The dog stopped scraping for a minute.

"Bow-wow, bow-wow-wow," he barked.

"Bow-wow. Bow-wow, indeed!" cried the little boy crossly.

"That's no name at all for a kitty."

So he crossed the pasture to the hill below, and he asked of the sheep who were grazing in a row,

"Sheep, what shall I call my kitty?"

"Baa," bleated all the sheep, raising their heads all in the same direction at the same time. "Baa."

"Baa," sighed the little boy. "I might have known. That's no name for a kitty."

So he went to the chickens to try his luck, but the chicks said, "Peep," and the hens said, "Cluck."

"And "Quack," said the duck when he asked the duck.

And the pig just grunted as if he hadn't heard.

And the fish in the fish pond *didn't say a word*.

So the little boy sat down sadly on the back doorstep in the sunlight and put his chin in his hands, and he thought and he thought and he thought.

The kitty chased a sunbeam and purred.

"Kitty," murmured the little boy. "Nice kitty.
Here, kitty, kitty, kitty."

And then all of a sudden he jumped up.

"I know!" he shouted happily. "I know what I'll call my kitty. I'll call her 'Kitty.'"
And he did.

Farmer Brown and his family live on a little farm
in the country.
   Every morning when the sun comes up,
Farmer Brown goes out to the barn.

He milks the cows.

He feeds hay to the horses.

He scatters grain to the hungry chickens.
"Cluck, cluck, cluck!" says the old red hen.

The pig likes to have his back scratched with a stick.
"Oink, oink," he grunts. He is very pleased.

When he has finished his chores, Farmer Brown
walks back to the farmhouse. Mrs. Brown cooks
eggs and bacon and pancakes for breakfast.

"Yum, yum!" say Sally and Sam. They are just as hungry as the animals on the farm. Jip and Mittens are hungry, too!

At nine o'clock, the school bus comes by to pick up Sally and Sam.

Honk! Honk! The driver toots the horn.

"Hi!" say all the children in the bus.

Sally and Sam climb in and wave goodbye to Jip as the bus drives down the road.

Farmer Brown goes back to the barn. He starts
up the tractor. It is time to cut and rake the hay.

He drives around the field in the warm sun.
Jip chases a rabbit in the tall grass.

In the farmhouse, Mrs. Brown is baking a chocolate cake. Aunt Alice and Uncle Tom are coming for supper.

They are bringing their two children to play with Sally and Sam.

Mittens wants to lick the bowl.

"Scat!" cries Mrs. Brown. Mittens is not really afraid, but he runs out the door.

It is noon, and time for lunch. Farmer Brown meets the mailman coming up the path. He has a package for the Browns.

What can it be?

Lots of new baby chicks! Farmer Brown carries the box out to the henhouse. When the chicks are bigger, they will run in the barnyard with the other farm animals.

At four o'clock, Sally and Sam come home from school.

They show Mrs. Brown their new books and pencils.

It's fun to play in the yard.
Sally climbs the apple tree, and Sam carves a
boat to sail on the pond.

The children ride their pony around the field.

Aunt Alice and Uncle Tom are here for supper.
Sally and Sam are glad to see their cousins.
Mrs. Brown's chocolate cake is a big success.
Uncle Tom eats three pieces!

The big folks sit and chat on the front porch
while the children play hide-and-go-seek. A harvest
moon is rising over the fields.

Aunt Alice and Uncle Tom and the children say
goodnight and drive away.

Time for bed! Tomorrow is another busy day.
Goodnight Sally. Goodnight Sam. Goodnight Jip
and Mittens.